Ruth M.

For OHR office

Bullfrog Pops!

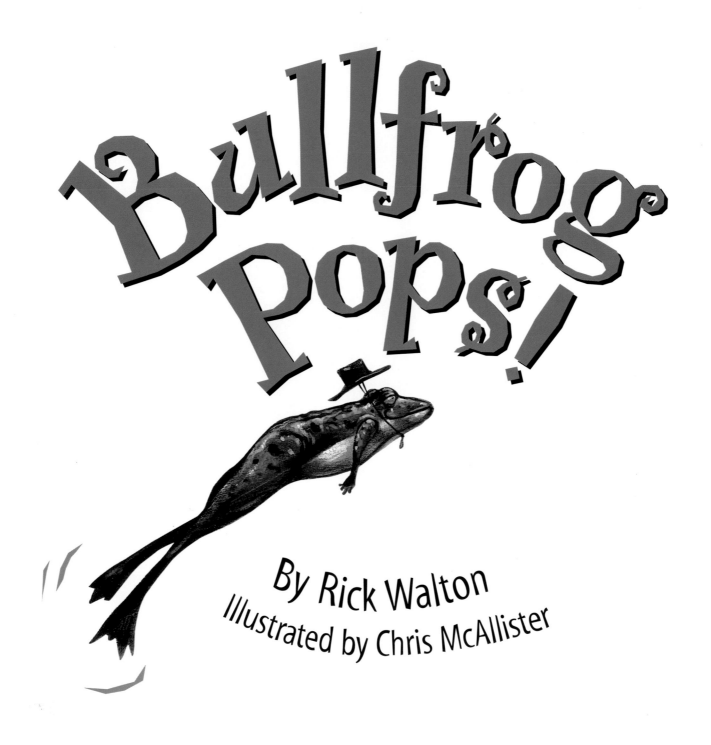

By Rick Walton
Illustrated by Chris McAllister

GIBBS·SMITH
P
PUBLISHER

Salt Lake City

To
Bob, Kris,
Meagen,
Jeremy, and Jacob Brown,
who will be welcome in any town.

R.W.

To Sean and Jamie for helping me
see life through the eyes of a child.

C.M.

03 02 01 00 99   5 4 3 2 1

Text copyright © 1999 Rick Walton
Illustrations copyright © 1999 by Chris McAllister

Published by
Gibbs Smith, Publisher
P.O. Box 667
Layton, Utah 84041

Orders: (1-800) 748-5439
Website: www.gibbs-smith.com

Edited by Suzanne Taylor
Book design and production by Denise Kirby
Printed and bound in Hong Kong

Library of Congress Cataloguing-in-Publication Data
Walton, Rick.
    Bullfrog pops! / Rick Walton; illustrated by Chris McAllister.
    p.   cm.
    Sequel to: Once there was a bull ... (frog).
    Summary: A hungry bullfrog hops a stagecoach to Ravenous Gulch where it tries
to get something to eat, in this tale where each page must be turned to complete the
sentence.
        ISBN 0-87905-903-6
        [1. Frogs—Fiction.] I. McAllister, Chris, 1958–   ill.
    II. Title.
PZ7.W1774Bu   1999
[E]—dc21   99-17216
                                                  CIP

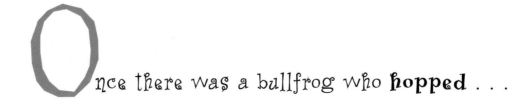

Once there was a bullfrog who **hopped** . . .

. . . **a stagecoach** and rode far away.
After many miles, he came to the town of Ravenous Gulch.

Bullfrog was hot. He was dirty.
He had not showered in many days.
And he **smelled** . . .

. . . **PIZZA!** Bullfrog was HUNGRY!
All he'd eaten for days was one horsefly.

He followed his nose to a sidewalk café
where a man sat eating a large, hot pizza.

"Name's Bullfrog," said Bullfrog. "Mind if I have a bite?"

"I'm Starvin' Marvin," said the pizza eater.
He held out his pizza. "Eat . . .

. . . **your heart out**, Bullfrog.
You're gettin' none of this!"

"That's not neighborly," said Bullfrog,
and he grabbed the pizza and leaped away.

"Give me back my pizza, you ornery varmint!"
yelled Starvin' Marvin. He chased Bullfrog.
Bullfrog tried to **hide** . . .

. . . **the pizza**, but
it was too big to hide, so he ate it. "Mmmmmm! RiBurp!"

"You pickle-skinned pizza thief!" yelled Starvin' Marvin.

"I'm still hungry!" yelled Bullfrog, as he leaped over
Starvin' Marvin and hopped away.

Bullfrog hopped to a garden where there was a large watermelon. Bullfrog loved watermelon so he picked it.

"HEY, YOU MELON-FILCHIN' FLY TRAP! PUT THAT DOWN!" said an old man with a pitchfork, running toward Bullfrog. Behind him was Starvin' Marvin. Bullfrog **dashed** . . .

. . . **the watermelon** to the ground
and gobbled up the juicy insides.
As the gardener and Starvin' Marvin drew closer,
Bullfrog leaped off.

"STOP HIM!" yelled the men.

"I'M STILL HUNGRY!" yelled Bullfrog.

He hopped until he came to a bakery.
"Ahhh! Bread!" said Bullfrog,
and he grabbed an armload and leaped out the door.
Then he heard the order. "HIT THE DIRT,
YOU LOAF-LIFTIN' COUSIN TO A GRASSHOPPER!"

Bullfrog turned. The baker was aiming a
slingshot at him. Bullfrog **dropped** . . .

. . . **the bread**, all but one big loaf,
which he ate as he raced down the street.

"STOP HIM!" yelled the baker.

"STOP HIM!" yelled the gardener and Starvin' Marvin.

"I'M STILL HUNGRY!" yelled Bullfrog.

$\mathcal{B}$ullfrog raced away. But when he looked back to see who was following him, WHAM! he ran into an apple tree.

"Ohhhhhh!" moaned Bullfrog. "Where am I?"

"You're in trouble, that's where you are," said Starvin' Marvin.

"Double trouble!" said the gardener.

"You're headin' to jail!" said the baker.

"You're under my apple tree!" said an old lady with pruning shears.

Bullfrog was surrounded. He began to **shake** . . .

. . . **the tree.**
Down fell apples. Bullfrog caught dozens in his mouth
and swallowed them. "STOP EATIN' MY APPLES,
YOU CANYON-MOUTHED FRUIT CATCHER!" shouted the old lady,
but Bullfrog jumped over her and away.

"STOP HIM!" yelled the people.

"I'M STILL HUNGRY!" yelled Bullfrog.

Bullfrog hopped until he came to the
Ravenous Gulch Fine Groceries, Fine Dining, and Fine Art Emporium.
The food inside smelled so good. He hopped inside and
looked out the door and down the street.
A crowd of people was racing toward him, waving weapons.
"Oh, no!" said Bullfrog, and he **bolted** . . .

. . . **the door shut** and began to eat.
He threw everything he could find into his mouth.
Hot dogs and hot tamales. French fries and fried chicken.
Soda pop and popcorn. Potato chips, chocolate chips,
even wood chips. He hopped so quickly from food to food
that the building shook and the
pictures fell from the walls.

And then Bullfrog noticed he wasn't alone.
Sitting quietly at one of the tables was the sheriff,
who stood up and rested his hand on his holster.
"Bullfrog," he said, "**draw** . . .

. . . *up a chair* to
my table and let's talk."
Bullfrog sat down.

"Now, Bullfrog," said the sheriff,
"what you've been doin' is serious.
You're gonna **hang** . . .

. . . those pictures back up."

"I see," said Bullfrog. "I **see** . . .

. . . **DOUGHNUTS!**" And he
grabbed one off the sheriff's plate and ate it.

The door burst open. In stormed Starvin' Marvin,
followed by the angry crowd.
"Where's my food?" roared Starvin' Marvin.
"How am I supposed to practice for the County Super Eater Contest?"
Starvin' Marvin grabbed a doughnut off the floor
and stuffed it in his mouth.

He began to **choke** . . .

. . . **Bullfrog**.

"STOP!" yelled the sheriff. "You're not thinkin' straight here, Marvin.
For twenty years you've tried to win that eatin' contest,
and we're mighty grateful for your effort.
But you've never won."

"This year, though," said the sheriff, "we're gonna enter
someone new, someone who can out-eat
anyone in the county. Why, he can out-eat anyone in the state
and probably the whole country.
Marvin, Bullfrog's gonna put Ravenous Gulch on the map!"

As the sheriff spoke, the townsfolk **gathered** . . .

. . . **food** for Bullfrog.

"Give him anything he wants!" they yelled.

"Great!" said Bullfrog, "because I'M STILL HUNGRY!"
And he started eating again.

"Does he look bigger to you?" asked the baker,
handing Bullfrog a plum pie.

"He won't burst, will he?" asked the old lady,
giving Bullfrog a basket of peaches.

"Just might," said the gardener,
handing Bullfrog a bunch of grapes.

And then, Bullfrog **POPPED** . . .

. . . **a grape** into his mouth and he was full.
"No more," he groaned.

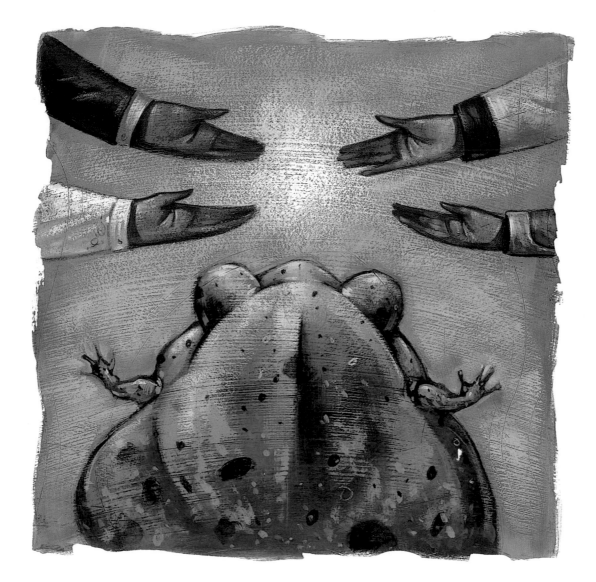

"Bullfrog," said the sheriff,
"because you've eaten so much of our food,
you're gonna have to **pay** . . .

. . . **us a visit** next week for the
County Super Eater Contest.
Come hungry."

And he did.